A Parents Magazine
Read Aloud Original

Sweet Dreams, Clown-Arounds!

by
Joanna Cole • **Jerry Smath**
pictures by

Parents Magazine Press
New York

Library of Congress Cataloging in Publication Data
Cole, Joanna.
    Sweet dreams, Clown-Arounds!
    Summary: After an exciting and busy day, the
Clown-Around family has trouble getting Baby to
go to bed.
    1. Children's stories, American. [1. Clowns—
Fiction. 2. Bedtime—Fiction] I. Smath, Jerry, ill.
II. Title.
PZ7.C67346Sw 1985   [E]   85-6348
ISBN 0-8193-1138-3

To Imogen—J.C.

To Kyle and Kendall Stratton—J.S.

It was a happy day
for Baby Clown-Around.

She went to the supermarket
with Mr. Clown-Around.

She went to the shoe store
with Mrs. Clown-Around.

She played with her
big sister, Bubbles,

and with Wag-Around, the dog.

Now it was Baby's bedtime.
Mr. Clown-Around fed her supper.

Mrs. Clown-Around helped her
brush her teeth.

And Bubbles and Wag-Around
kissed her good night.

But Baby had had such
a happy day that she
did not want to go to sleep.

So she played a trick
on the Clown-Arounds.

"Where is Baby?"
Mrs. Clown-Around
asked.

Mrs. Clown-Around looked
in her teacup.
Baby was not there.

Mr. Clown-Around looked
in his shoe.

And Bubbles looked in the fishbowl.
But they could not find Baby.

Then Wag-Around followed his nose.
There was Baby!

"Now it is really bedtime,"
said Mrs. Clown-Around.

She tucked Baby in.

But Baby did not go to sleep.
"Wah, wah!" she cried.

Mr. Clown-Around rocked
the cradle,
but it didn't help.

Wag-Around sang a lullaby,
but that woke Baby up
even more.

Mrs. Clown-Around looked for
an extra blanket in the closet,
but that made things worse than ever.

Even Bubbles couldn't
put Baby to sleep.

All at once,
Baby reached out her hands
and said, "Bear!"

"No wonder she can't sleep!"
said Mr. Clown-Around.

He rushed out...

and brought back
a big bear.

But Baby didn't want it anymore.
"Monkey!" she said.

"She needs a monkey too!"
said Mrs. Clown-Around.
Mrs. Clown-Around rushed out...

and came back with a monkey.

But Baby didn't want it.
"Horse!" she said.

"I know where to get one,"
said Bubbles.

By the time Bubbles
came back with the horse,
Baby had stopped crying.

She was reading
a good-night book to herself.

Mr. Clown-Around
listened to the story,
and his eyes began to close.

Baby turned out the bright light.
It was so restful in the dark,
that Mrs. Clown-Around dozed off.

Baby hummed a little bedtime tune,
and Bubbles and Wag-Around
fell asleep.

Baby looked around.
The whole family
was fast asleep!

She covered them up.
Then Baby went to sleep too.

The Clown-Arounds think that
the best ending to a happy day
is a good night's sleep.
Don't you?

About the Author

JOANNA COLE and her family recently had an experience similar to the one in this book when they got a new puppy. Muffy slept a lot during the day and was wide awake at bedtime. "We tried everything to get her to sleep," said the author. "But just like Baby, she wouldn't sleep until she had tired herself out."

Joanna Cole has written many books for children, including five about the Clown-Around family. She lives in New York City with her husband, daughter, and two Yorkshire terriers.

About the Artist

JERRY SMATH does free-lance illustration for magazines and children's school books. He has written and illustrated four books for Parents in addition to illustrating the Clown-Around series. "It's been a lot of fun bringing the Clown-Arounds to life," says Mr. Smath. "I hope I've done justice to Joanna's lively imagination."

Mr. Smath and his wife, Valerie, a graphic designer, live in Westchester County, New York.